MARIAJO ILUSTRAJO

FLOODED

WE NEED TO DO SOMETHING

THE CITY WOKE UP, JUST AS
ON ANY OTHER SUMMER'S DAY.

FLOODED

To my lovely friends and tutors at Anglia Ruskin who were with me at the beginning of this journey and to my amazing team at Quarto who brought my first book to life.
– M.I.

The Quarto Group
Inspiring | Educating | Creating | Entertaining

Brimming with creative inspiration, how-to projects, and useful information to enrich your everyday life, quarto.com is a favourite destination for those pursuing their interests and passions.

Text and Illustration © 2022 Mariajo Ilustrajo

First published in 2023 by First Editions, an initiative of Frances Lincoln Children's Books, an imprint of The Quarto Group, The Old Brewery, 6 Blundell Street, London N7 9BH, United Kingdom. T (0)20 7700 6700 F (0)20 7700 8066 www.Quarto.com

The right of Mariajo Ilustrajo to be identified as the author and illustrator of this work has been asserted by them in accordance with the Copyright, Designs and Patents Act, 1988 (United Kingdom).

ISBN 978-0-7112-7679-6
eISBN 978-0-7112-7680-2

Illustrated in ink and edited digitally
Set in Simone and Perfect Match

Published by Katie Cotton & Peter Marley
Commissioned and edited by Lucy Brownridge
Designed by Zoë Tucker
Production by Dawn Cameron

Manufactured in Guangdong, China TT092022
9 8 7 6 5 4 3 2 1

MIX
Paper from responsible sources
FSC® C016973
www.fsc.org

ALTHOUGH SOMETHING
WAS DIFFERENT.

IT WASN'T A PROBLEM.

THE CITY WAS
JUST A BIT...

NOBODY SEEMED TO MIND A LITTLE BIT OF WATER. IT WAS A GREAT EXCUSE TO WEAR WELLIES!

Excuse me...

THE CITY CARRIED ON
IN ITS USUAL RHYTHM.
GOING UP,
GOING DOWN.
AFTER ALL, IT WAS JUST
A BIT OF WATER.

IT WAS SOMETHING TO TALK ABOUT AT WORK.

AND SCHOOL
HAD NEVER BEEN
SO MUCH FUN.

THE WATER KEPT ON RISING.
STILL, MOST PEOPLE DIDN'T SEEM TO MIND.
THEY KNEW IT WOULD GO AWAY SOON.

BUT FOR THE SMALLER ANIMALS,

IS WAS BECOMING HARDER
AND HARDER TO COPE.

THE LITTLE BIT OF WATER WAS BECOMING A
HUGE PROBLEM, AND IT WASN'T GOING AWAY.

WHERE WAS THE WATER COMING FROM?
AND WHAT COULD THEY DO ABOUT IT?

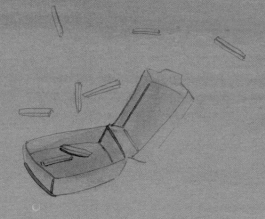

...EXCEPT FOR A LITTLE SOMEONE
WHO HAD KNOWN FROM THE BEGINNING.
IF ONLY THE OTHERS HAD LISTENED TO
HIM, THE PROBLEM WOULD NEVER HAVE
BECOME SO HUGE. THE SOLUTION
WAS SIMPLE...

BUT IT WASN'T A JOB FOR ONE!
EVERYONE HAD TO WORK TOGETHER.

AND ONCE THEY DID...

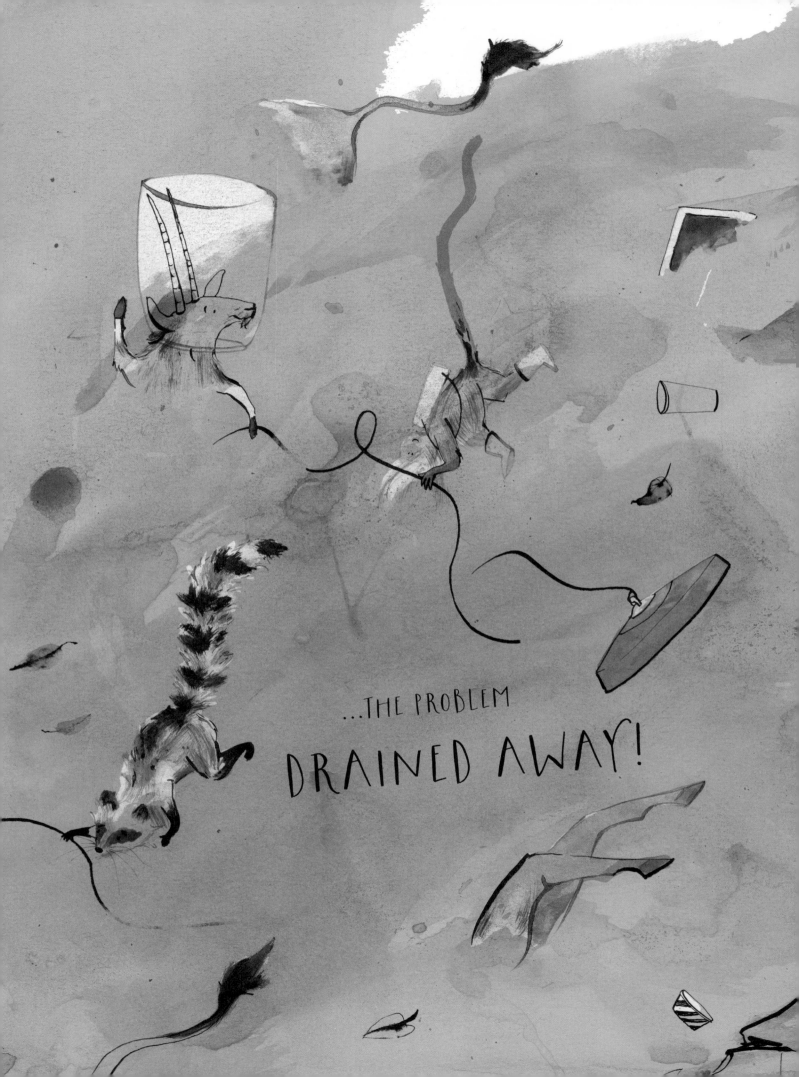

...THE PROBLEM

DRAINED AWAY!

NOTHING WAS QUITE THE
SAME AS BEFORE.

THERE WERE LOTS OF
NEW PROBLEMS.

BUT NOW THEY KNEW
THE ONLY WAY TO FIX
A PROBLEM...

WAS TOGETHER.